Follow the Swallow

Julia Donaldson

Illustrated by Martin Ursell

Other titles in the bunch:

Big Dog and Little Dog Go Sailing
Big Dog and Little Dog Visit the Moon
Colin and the Curly Claw
Dexter's Journey
Follow the Swallow
"Here I Am!" said Smedley

Horrible Haircut
Magic Lemonade
The Magnificent Mummies
Midnight in Memphis
Peg
Shoot!

Crabtree Publishing Company
www.crabtreebooks.com

PMB 16A, 350 Fifth Avenue
Suite 3308
New York, NY 10118

612 Welland Avenue
St. Catharines, Ontario
Canada, L2M 5V6

Donaldson, Julia.
　Follow the swallow / Julia Donaldson ; illustrated by Martin Ursell.
　　p. cm. -- (Blue Bananas)
Summary: As one creature passes it on to the next, Chack the
blackbird's message to his friend Apollo the swallow undergoes major
changes.
　　ISBN 0-7787-0842-X -- ISBN 0-7787-0888-8 (pbk.)
　[1. Communication--Fiction. 2. Birds--Fiction. 3. Animals--Fiction.
4. Friendship--Fiction.] I. Ursell, Martin, ill. II. Title. III. Series.
PZ7.D71499 Fo 2002
[E]--dc21
　　　　　　　　　　　2001032441
　　　　　　　　　　　LC

Published by Crabtree Publishing in 2002
First published in 2000 by Mammoth
an imprint of Egmont Children's Books Limited
Text copyright © Julia Donaldson 2000
Illustrations © Martin Ursell 2000
The Author and Illustrator have asserted their moral rights.
Paperback ISBN 0-7787-0888-8
Reinforced Hardcover Binding ISBN 0-7787-0842-X

Follow the Swallow

Julia Donaldson

Illustrated by Martin Ursell

BLue Bananas

For Helen
J.D.

For Anne
M.U.

Chack the blackbird was learning to fly.

So was Apollo the swallow.

That was how they met.

"Who are you?" asked Chack.

"I'm Apollo. I'm a swallow."

"And what do you swallow?"

"Flies, mostly," said Apollo. "And who are you?"

I love flies!

"I'm Chack. I'm a blackbird."

"You look brown to me," said Apollo.

"I may be brown now but one day I'll
be black," said Chack.

"I don't believe you!" said Apollo.

Apollo showed Chack his nest. It was

on a cobwebby shelf in a shed.

"I won't always live here," he said.

"One day I'll fly away to Africa."

"I don't believe you!" said Chack.

Chack showed Apollo his nest. It was

in a tree covered in white blossoms.

"One day the tree will be covered in tasty orange berries," said Chack.

"I don't believe you!" said Apollo.

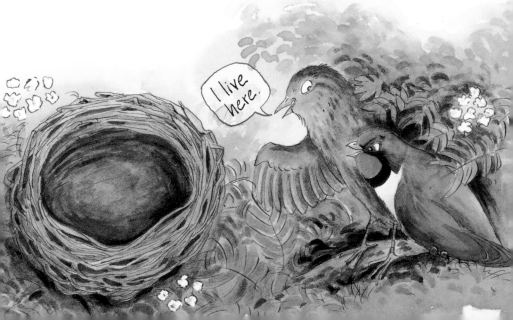

The days grew longer and warmer.
Apollo started hanging around with a lot
of other swallows. They kept gathering
on the roof of the shed and then flying
off all together.

"What are you doing?" asked Chack.

"Practicing flying to Africa!" said Apollo.

"I don't believe you!" said Chack.

The white blossoms fell off Chack's tree

and some little green berries appeared.

"They'll be orange one day," he told Apollo.

"I don't believe you!"

said Apollo.

Slowly the berries on the tree grew bigger and changed color, from green . . . to yellow . . . and at last to orange.

"Now Apollo will believe me!" said Chack. He flew to the shed to tell his friend about the orange berries.

"Come to the tree! Come to the tree!" he called.

I can't wait to show Apollo!

But Apollo had gone. He and the other swallows had just set off for Africa.

Chack flew after the swallows. He flew
and he flew until he reached the sea.
There he met a leaping dolphin.

"Can you take a message to Apollo the swallow from Chack the blackbird?" asked Chack. "He's on his way to Africa."

"What is the message?" asked the dolphin.

"Come to the tree!" said Chack, and he

flew back to eat some of the tasty orange

berries.

The leaping dolphin swam and jumped and dived.

It took him a long time to reach Africa.

There he met a grumpy camel.

"Can you take a message to Apollo the swallow from Chack the blackbird?" asked the dolphin.

Hey, grumpy!

"What's the message?" asked the camel.

"Er . . . er . . . Jump in the sea!" said the dolphin.

The grumpy camel trudged slowly across the desert . . .

. . . until he reached a wide river. There he met a hungry crocodile.

"Can you take a message to Apollo the swallow from Chack the blackbird?" asked the camel.

"What's the message?" asked the crocodile.

"Er . . . er . . . Grumpy like me!" said the camel.

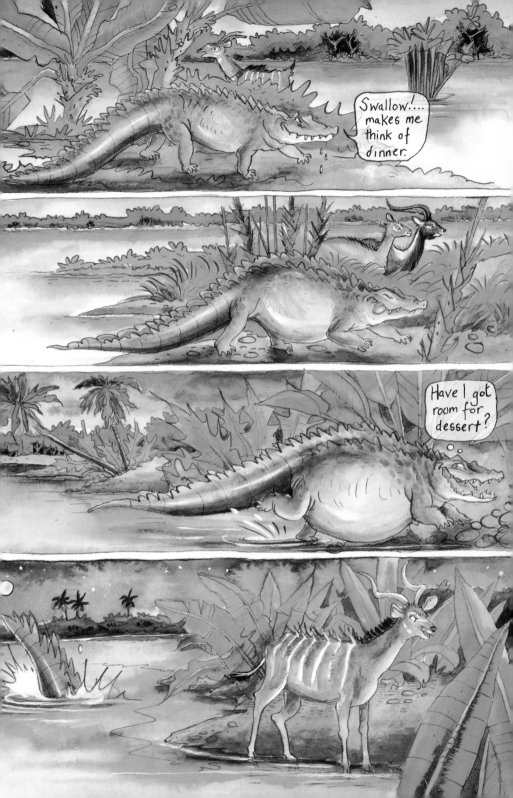

The hungry crocodile took his time

swimming and snapping his way down

the river . . . until he came to a forest.

There he met a playful monkey.

"Can you take a message to Apollo
the swallow from Chack the blackbird?"
asked the crocodile.

Monkey
for me

"What is the message?" asked the monkey.

"Er. . . er . . . Monkey for me!" said the
crocodile.

The playful monkey swung from branch
to branch until he came to a fig tree . . .

On the ground lay a lot of rotten figs.

Feeding on the rotten figs were a lot of

fruit flies, and snapping at the fruit flies

were a lot of swallows.

"I've got a message for Apollo the swallow," said the monkey.

"That's me!" said one of the swallows. "What is the message and who is it from?"

"It's from Chack the blackbird and the

message is . . . er, er, One, two, three,

whee!" said the monkey.

33

"One, two, three, whee!" said Apollo.

"That's a funny message! Well, I've been in Africa for half a year now. It's time for me to fly back to the garden. I can find out what Chack means."

Apollo and the other swallows flew back,

over the forest . . .

and the river . . .

and the desert . . .

Monkey for me..

Grumpy like me!

and the sea . . .

Jump in the sea.

Nearly home now.

. . . until they reached the garden. Apollo flew to Chack's tree. It was covered in white blossoms.

A big blackbird flew down from the tree.

"I'm looking for my friend Chack," said

Apollo.

"That's me!" said Chack.

"I don't believe you!"

said Apollo.

You're not Chack!

"You're black and Chack was brown."

"I'm Chack as sure as eggs are eggs," said Chack. "And speaking of eggs, I've got something to show you."

He flew up to a nest in the tree. Apollo
flew after him. A brown bird was sitting
in the nest.

"Time for your worm-break, Rowena,"
said Chack.

The brown bird flew off, and there in the nest Apollo saw some pale, blue-green eggs. He counted them . . . "one, two, three. So the message wasn't: one, two, three, whee! It was: one, two, three eggs!" he said.

"No, it wasn't!" said Chack. "It was:

come to the tree!"

"Well, I have come to the tree and I've

seen the eggs, and I think they're

beautiful," said Apollo.

The message was. "Come to the tree!"

"But the message wasn't about the eggs,

it was about the orange berries," said Chack.

"Orange berries! Orange berries! You're

not still talking about orange berries, are

you?" Apollo started to laugh.

"But there really were orange berries!"
said Chack. "There were and there will
be again."

Apollo thought hard. "All right," he said,

"I believe you."

Did you spot these animals?